Robin Hood

Retold by
Stewart Ross

Illustrated by
Alex Paterson

ARCTURUS

For Ruby Pietrasik, with much love—SR.

For Eva and Nate—AP.

ARCTURUS

This edition published in 2018 by Arcturus Publishing Limited
26/27 Bickels Yard, 151–153 Bermondsey Street,
London SE1 3HA

Writer: Stewart Ross
Illustrator: Alex Paterson
Designer: Jeni Child
Editor: Sebastian Rydberg
Art Director: Jessica Crass

ISBN: 978-1-78828-688-6
CH006282NT
Supplier 24, Date 0318, Print run 6732

Printed in Malaysia

Contents

CHAPTER 1

Robin Hood the Outlaw

Long ago, when the rich lived in stone castles and the poor in wooden huts, all was not well in England. Good King Richard had gone overseas to fight his enemies, and the kingdom was in the hands of his cruel brother, Prince John.

John had no interest in caring for his people. He allowed the powerful to bully the weak. He looked the other way as bishops and abbots grew richer, while peasants starved. Taxes went up, and misery spread through the land like a disease.

One man fought bravely against this evil. He robbed from the rich to give to the poor; he defended the weak; he challenged the bullies, breaking their greasy heads

and bringing down their flinty castles.

The name of this man was Robin Hood.

Robin's real name was Robert of
Locksley, a young, well-to-do farmer of
rich lands. But the monks of the Abbey of
St. Mary looked with greedy eyes on these
lands. If Robert were declared an outlaw,
they plotted, they could seize his farm.

Fortunately for them, Robert of Locksley
played into the hands of the wicked
monks. He made himself an outlaw.

Robert became an outlaw because he fought for justice. He returned from a long journey to find that the man who looked after the abbey lands, Sir Guy of Gisborne, was treating the families who lived there most cruelly. Gisborne threw peasants out of their houses, stole money and women, and killed those who disobeyed him.

When Robert heard what was happening, he was mad with anger. His fury became unstoppable when he learned that his friend, Will Scarlet, was chained in Gisborne's prison. "Enough is enough!" Robert cried. "Follow me to end the rule of this devil Gisborne!"

Commanded by Robert of Locksley, the villagers attacked Gisborne's soldiers and killed many of them with arrows.

When they burned
Gisborne's house,
he just managed to
escape on horseback
into the night.

After that, Robert of Locksley was
known as Robin Hood, the outlaw.
Now that he had broken the law, he was
outside the law's protection. He was a
"wolf's head": Anyone was allowed to
capture or kill him. But no one did.

Robin led his band of trusty followers
deep into Sherwood Forest. There, safe
from bullying lords and priests, they

continued to
fight beside Robin
for generosity,
fairness, and
justice.

Robin Hood wished to marry his true love, the beautiful Maid Marian. She felt the same about him.

But her father was an earl, and marriage between ordinary people and nobles was frowned upon.

Robin had a rival for Marian's hand: the proud knight, Roger de Longchamp. *If Marian won't marry me for love,* Roger said to himself, *I'll capture her and marry her by force!*

So, when Marian came riding through Sherwood Forest one day, Roger ambushed her. "Come, my fair lady!" he mocked. "I'll find a priest to make you my wife."

Before the words left his mouth, a

humming echoed through the forest. It was an arrow, an arrow from the mighty bow of Robin Hood. Straight and true it flew, through the eyeholes in de Longchamp's helmet and into his head. He swayed, then fell from his horse. He was dead.

"Oh, Robin!" cried Marian, throwing her arms around him. "You have saved me from a monster. How can I thank you?"

"Marry me, and live with me in the forest," he replied with a merry smile.

"Alas, not until my father agrees," she said and went on her way with a heavy heart.

Those who wished to join Robin's outlaw band in Sherwood Forest had to promise to follow these rules:

1. Protect all women.
2. Protect all honest peasants.
3. Treat all unproud knights kindly.
4. Steal from rich priests, and give the money to the poor.

One man who accepted these rules was Alan de Tranmire, a young squire known to his friends as Alan-a-Dale. He met Robin when the outlaws were praying in church. Hob o' the Hill, one of Robin's tiny woodland friends, sneaked in and whispered a warning in Robin's ear. "Soldiers of your worst enemy, Sir Isenbart de Belame, have followed you!"

When the enemy attacked, Robin's men were ready for them. The furious

fight was soon over, and all but one of
de Belame's men lay dead. The one still
living was Ivo le Ravener.

"Leave him to me," cried Alan-a-Dale.
They fought long and hard, but in the end,
the older knight tired, and Alan's sword
pierced his heart. Thus were the merry men
of Sherwood Forest joined by yet another
brave and honest fighter, Alan-a-Dale.

Two days later, a second famous warrior joined Robin's band. His name was John o' the Stubbs—though the outlaws called him something different. Here's why.

Wandering through the forest, Robin and Alan-a-Dale found Grim Jake, a hated forester, bound up in front of his hut. When Jake said that he had been tied up for refusing to share his meal with a stranger, Robin cried, "I'd like to meet this admirable stranger!"

Not long afterward, he did.

Robin was crossing a broad, fast-flowing stream on a tree-trunk bridge when an enormous man appeared on the other bank. He was dressed like a peasant and carried a massive staff.

"Out of my way, little man, or I'll walk over you!" he roared, with a twinkle in his eye.

When Robin refused to step aside,
the man sprang onto the oak bridge
and attacked him with his staff. Thwack!
Crack! The pair rained blows on each
other, until, with a mighty swipe, the giant
sent Robin spinning into the river.

"What a fighter!" laughed the soaking-
wet Robin, as he dragged himself to the
bank. "Join my outlaw band, mighty fellow."
He did—and they called him Little John.

CHAPTER 2
The Sheriff of Nottingham

By now, Robin Hood's reputation had spread far beyond Nottinghamshire. His men were also famous: Alan-a-Dale, Will Scarlet, and Little John.

Hob o' the Hill told of another brave man who ought to join them: Friar Tuck.

One spring morning, Robin met Peter the Doctor in the forest. Peter, who sold useless medicines, told Robin of his meeting with the hefty friar. The rogue had forced him to eat all his own medicines—and they had made him ill!

Robin roared with laughter. *I must meet this jolly rogue*, he thought. He found Tuck sitting beside a stream.

"Hey, holy man," Robin called, raising

his bow, "You look strong. Carry me across the water on your back!"

Tuck stood up slowly, waded over to Robin, and carried him back to the other side. Then, quick as an arrow, he grabbed Robin. "My turn now," he grinned. "Carry me across on your back!"

Robin saw the joke and carried the heavy friar to the other side. After that, they were best of friends, and Friar Tuck joined Robin's outlaws.

A few months later, Robin received a warning from his cousin, Master Gammell. "Ralph Murdach, Sheriff of Nottingham, is hatching a plot with Sir Guy of Gisborne," Gammell told him.

"They'll send spies dressed as beggars into the forest. Since you treat the poor well, they'll learn your secret hiding places. The soldiers will then attack."

Robin thanked his cousin warmly. Remembering the warning, he was suspicious when he met a sturdy beggar on a forest track. The fellow looked as if he were acting and his eyes moved shiftily from side to side.

Robin asked what he was doing. The so-called beggar became angry. Without warning, he swiped Robin over the head with his staff and ran off. Two outlaws

gave chase and caught up with him.

Searching the villain, they found a
money bag and a letter. As they were
examining the letter, the villain reached
inside his cloak, took out a bag of flour,
and threw the dust in the outlaws' eyes.
They were too blinded to follow, and he
escaped once again.

"Sorry, Robin," they said when they
returned to their camp, "but we got the
money. And the letter might be interesting."

Robin's face turned grim as he read the letter. It came from Sir Guy of Gisborne and was addressed to the Sheriff of Nottingham. It read: "Richard Illbeast, the man bringing this letter, is a crafty devil who can lead us to the secret camp of that wolf's head, Robin Hood."

"Right, Sheriff," muttered Robin when he had finished reading the letter, "instead of you coming here, I'm going to pay you a visit."

The next day, Robin disguised himself

as a potter and rode into Nottingham on a borrowed horse and cart. He sold his pots at such low prices that even the sheriff's wife bought some. To thank him for the bargain, she invited him to dine at the sheriff's table.

No one recognized the outlaw, and he enjoyed a hearty meal. When it was over, Richard Illbeast appeared. He had been set upon by a dozen outlaws in the forest, he lied. They had stolen his money and the letter he was bringing for the sheriff.

"Idiot!" sneered the sheriff. "Made a fool of by Robin Hood? Out of my house!"

Robin grinned at Illbeast's reception. Moments later, he grinned again: The sheriff was proposing an archery contest.

The sheriff looked surprised when Robin said he'd like to enter the competition. "Whoever heard of a potter with a bow and arrow?" he mocked. "But you can try your luck if you want."

"Thank you, sire," replied Robin politely.

The sheriff's men shot straight and true, but the potter shot straighter and truer. Those watching were astonished. By the third round, only two men were left in the competition: Robin and the sheriff's crack shot.
Robin won easily.

"Good heavens!" cried the sheriff, when he saw how well the potter handled his bow. "Where on earth did you learn to shoot like that?"

"Excuse me, sire," said Robin, "but I once shot with Robin Hood."

Murdach's face darkened. "Robin Hood, the wolf's head?" he asked suspiciously. "I hope you're not one of his band?"

"No, sire!" assured Robin, shaking his head. "I don't like that outlaw any more than you do. In fact, for a reward, I can lead you to his camp in the forest."

"Done!" growled Sheriff Murdach. "A hundred pounds for you, potter, if you will take me to that pesky Hood fellow."

"Nothing would give me greater pleasure," replied Robin, smiling calmly.

The following day dawned dark and damp. Sheriff Murdach took thirty armed soldiers and rode with the potter into Sherwood Forest. The farther they went, the gloomier it became.

Sinister howls and shrieks came from between the trees. "The forest spirits are coming," cried the soldiers and fled.

Soon, the potter was the sheriff's only companion. A horn rang out. As if by magic, twenty men with bows at the ready appeared on either side of the path.

"All well, potter?" grinned Little John.

"Fine, thank you!" replied Robin. "I've brought the sheriff along to have dinner with us." He turned to face his prisoner. "Well, Sheriff, I've kept my word, haven't I? You've now met Robin Hood!"

Murdach scowled as the forest echoed

to the outlaws' laughter.

A great feast was prepared. The main dish was venison from the forest deer that the sheriff and his foresters were paid to protect. Murdach ate with a sour face.

After the meal, the sheriff's money, arms, and other valuable possessions were taken from him. Little John then lifted him onto a pony, seated backward, and sent him on his way to Nottingham.

CHAPTER 3

Justice for Richard Illbeast

Of all Robin Hood's enemies, the most wicked was Sir Isenbart de Belame. Such terrible things were done in his castle that the peasants called it Evil Hold.

Alan-a-Dale had a special reason to hate the master of Evil Hold. He dearly wished to marry the young Lady Alice. Sir Isenbart de Belame had other ideas.

He threatened to take all the lands belonging to Alan's father, Sir Herbrand. The knight could keep them only if he gave Alice to Sir Ranulf de Greasby, one of de Belame's nasty old friends.

Eventually, Sir Herbrand agreed that Alice could marry the fifty-three-year-old Sir Ranulf. Maid Marian, poor Alice's dear friend, told Robin what was going on—and the outlaw sprang into action.

He disguised himself and led a band of his men to the church. The priest, who had been bullied into performing the ceremony, looked miserable. Alice was crying. Only Sir Ranulf looked pleased.

As the service began, Robin threw off his disguise and ordered the wedding to stop. Before Sir Ranulf could react, he fell dead with an arrow in his throat.

A tremendous battle began. Arrows flew and swords clashed, as the outlaws fought Sir Ranulf's soldiers and friends.

The fiercest fight was between Robin and Sir Ector de Malstane. The villain fought well, but Robin was more skilled. After killing him, Robin turned to see Sir Philip de Scrooby picking up Alice and carrying her off. Robin dashed to the rescue.

The outlaws caught Sir Philip before he got away. Free at last, Alice fell into the arms of Alan. Three weeks later, the couple were married by Friar Tuck beneath the trees of Sherwood Forest.

*

On the evening of the battle, Sir Isenbart de Belame had been at dinner in Evil Hold. With him were his foul friends: Sir Niger le Grym, Hamo de Mortain, and

Baldwin the Killer. They were waiting for Sir Ranulf and his bride to join them.

Suddenly, a black arrow thudded into the table in front of them. On it, written in blood, was a message:

These are dead—Roger de Longchamp, Ivo le Ravener, Sir Ranulf de Greasby, Sir Ector de Malstane, Sir Philip de Scrooby.

These shall die—Niger le Grym, Hamo de Mortain, Baldwin the Killer—and Sir Isenbart de Belame.

Sir Isenbart de Belame ranted and raged, but he never learned who shot the arrow into his table. Robin knew it was Hob o' the Hill, the only man able to sneak into Evil Hold unnoticed.

Meanwhile, the outlaws continued their struggle against wicked men. Robin collected money from the rich who passed through Sherwood Forest. Most of it he gave to the poor, but some he saved.

Sir Herbrand was in trouble again. The greedy monks of St. Mary's Abbey demanded four hundred pounds in rent for his lands.

"Pay within a year," cackled Abbot Robert, the head of the abbey, "or your lands will be ours." He knew that Sir Herbrand did not have the money.

The knight turned to Robin for help. The outlaw willingly lent him four hundred pounds, and Abbot Robert's plan failed. He was furious—but could do nothing.

Will Stuteley, one of Robin's most trusted followers, was also helping the poor and weak. One day in the forest, he met a little girl— Ruth. She was sobbing as she picked flowers to cheer herself up.

She led Will to her father, whose name was Ruben. "What has happened?" Will asked. "Why are you alone in the wild forest?"

Ruben explained how he and his people
living in the city of York had been
attacked. Their treasure had
been stolen, their houses
burned, and many killed.

"But why?" asked Will.

"Because we belong to
the Jewish race," Ruben
said sadly. "We did nothing wrong."

When Will heard who had led the
attack on the Jewish people, his blood
ran cold. It was that monster, Richard
Illbeast, again!

Will asked how he could help. Ruben
wondered whether the outlaw would go
into Nottingham and tell the Jews there
that he and Ruth were safe. Ruben didn't
dare do this himself because Illbeast was
in the city.

Without a moment's hesitation, Will agreed to do as Ruben asked. He disguised himself as a pilgrim and went into Nottingham. After delivering the message, he was resting at an inn, when one of the sheriff's soldiers seized him.

"Excellent!" he cried. "We've got one of Robin Hood's outlaws at last! My master will be delighted."

Sheriff Murdach was indeed delighted. "Hang him!" he ordered, when Will was brought before him. "Hang him in the square tomorrow!"

Will's friends hurried to Robin Hood with the dreadful news. When he heard it, Robin uttered just one word: "Rescue!"

At dawn, the sheriff's men brought Will into the main square. He looked at the wooden gallows and sighed. *Not even Robin Hood can save me now, he thought.*

He was wrong. The captain in charge of the hanging grinned cruelly and shouted, "Right, men! One, two …"

All at once, a stone whistled through the air and knocked the captain senseless, Little John cut Will free, and Robin's archers rained arrows onto the guards.

Sheriff Murdach was furious. "Bring more men from the castle," he screamed.

Before they arrived, Robin and his men had disappeared. Finding that the captain was none other than villainous Richard Illbeast, they had taken him with them.

On their way back through the forest, the outlaws found an important-looking man on horseback blocking their path. "Give me your prisoner!" he commanded.

Robin refused. "Who are you?"

"I am the King's Justice," he replied. "Illbeast is wanted for many foul crimes."

"In which case," suggested Robin, "shall we punish him together, now?"

The Justice agreed. A rope was slung over the bough of a tree. Moments later, Richard Illbeast, one of the nastiest criminals in all England, met his end.

CHAPTER 4
The Archery Contest

A year went by. While Robin Hood waited patiently to marry Maid Marian, he and the outlaws continued to rob the rich and give to the poor. But three wealthy bullies remained beyond their grasp: Isenbart de Belame, the Sheriff, and Abbot Robert.

One spring morning, things changed. As Robin was wondering when Sir Herbrand would repay his debt, Little John appeared with two fat prisoners. He had captured Abbot Robert and the monk who controlled the abbey larder.

Robin searched the saddlebags of his captives' horses, bringing out handfuls of coins. "My four hundred pounds! Thanks, good Abbot!"

The abbot fumed and swore and called Robin all kinds of awful names. The outlaws tied him to a tree and invited him to join their feast. He was too angry and embarrassed to eat much.

After the meal, Little John tied the abbot to his horse and sent him off. The larder monk walked beside him. Everyone they met, including the monks of the abbey, roared with laughter at the sight.

Abbot Robert never got over his shame, and the following spring he died.

The passing of Abbot Robert should have been good news for Robin Hood, but it wasn't. Sir Isenbart de Belame got his nephew, Robert de Longchamp, chosen as the new abbot. The two men plotted with Sir Guy of Gisborne and Sheriff Murdach to get rid of Robin and his outlaws once and for all.

The sheriff remembered the archery contest Robin had won when disguised as a potter. "I'm trying it again," he said with a sneer. "I'm offering first prize of a silver arrow tipped with pure gold."

"That wretched outlaw loves gold, and he's proud of his shooting. He's bound to turn up—and this time, we'll be waiting for him!"

He was right. Robin couldn't resist the idea of an archery contest. He suspected a plot, so he disguised himself as a vagabond. He told six other outlaw archers to enter the contest, with more to be in the crowd in case of trouble.

The day came, and eager spectators thronged the Nottingham meadows. Archers from all over the country had entered, all hoping to win the gold and silver arrow. The fine lords and ladies took their seats, a trumpet blared, and the contest began.

The first test was for each archer to fire three arrows at a target fifty yards away. Those who failed to get two arrows inside the bull had to drop out. The target was then moved farther back. More dropped out.

By the time the target was three hundred yards away, only twenty archers remained. The crowd became very excited when the large target was replaced by a thin wooden pole. Soon, there were only six archers left in the competition: Robin, Little John, Scadlock, Much the Miller's son, Reynold, and Luke the Red.

The shooting became even more difficult when the archers were not told the distance to the pole. Having worked it out for themselves, they had to select the right bow and arrow for that range.

After two more rounds, only Robin
Hood and Luke the Red remained. Luke
was the sheriff's man.

For the final round, Robin and Luke
had just three seconds to raise their bow,
fit an arrow, aim, and fire. Luke went first.
The crowd held their breath … He missed!

Next came Robin, disguised as a tramp:
one … two … three … The crowd gasped
in astonishment. Robin's arrow had split
the pole in two!

As the sheriff's
wife presented Robin
with the precious
arrow, her husband
peered closely at him.
Suddenly, he cried out, "It's Robin Hood,
the outlaw! Arrest him!"

Robin raised his horn and blew a
clear blast. Immediately, thirty armed
outlaws sprang to his side. Seeing this,
the sheriff's herald blew his trumpet,
and sixty of Murdach's men surrounded
Robin and his band.

Though the fight was furious, the
outnumbered outlaws eventually gained
the upper hand. But before they could
claim victory, a hundred more of the
sheriff's soldiers came riding out of
Nottingham Castle.

Robin ordered his men to fall back to a clump of trees. There, they would fight to the last. At that moment, a tiny figure appeared at Robin's side. It was Ket the Trow, the brother of Hob o' the Hill.

"Quick, Robin," panted Ket. "I come from Maid Marian's father, Sir Richard at the Lee. He offers you shelter in his castle nearby."

"But if he helps me, he will be declared an outlaw," said Robin.

"He cares not,'" replied Ket. "Come, follow me."

In the nick of time, Robin led his band to the safety of Verysdale Castle, where Sir Richard welcomed them most warmly.

Sir Richard told Robin that Maid Marian was staying with her aunt in Malaset Castle. "But she won't be safe now that Murdach is your enemy," cried Robin. "I'll go to her at once."

When he reached Malaset, his heart sank. Marian was gone.

"Sir Scrivel of Catsty has taken her away," explained a tearful maid. "He said that because Marian's father is an outlaw, he'll protect her by marrying her."

"Never!" cried Robin. "Sir Scrivel's a vile dog who wouldn't protect anyone!"

For days, he hunted for his dearest Marian. He searched in towns and in the countryside, in fields and in woods, but all in vain. He returned to Sherwood Forest to wait for news.

Three days later, Sheriff Murdach passed

nearby. He was escorting a prisoner—Sir
Richard at the Lee. Without hesitation,
Robin ambushed the soldiers and set Sir
Richard free. "Now, Sheriff," said Robin
grimly, "it is time to meet your end."

His swift arrow pierced the villain's
chest plate and entered his heart.

Robin found Marian shortly afterward.
She was happily asleep in the burrow
home of Ket the Trow. "But how … ?"

Ket smiled. "Just be happy she's here."

CHAPTER 5

Robin and King Richard

Now that Sir Richard was also an outlaw, his daughter was free to marry her love. With her father's permission, Maid Marian said "yes" to Robin, and Friar Tuck married them beneath an oak tree.

Robin and Marian lived with their friends in the forest for several years. As

before, they protected the poor and weak, and punished bullies and lawbreakers.

But good King Richard was still absent. At home, Prince John continued to govern England with a cruel and careless hand. The people longed for their king to return and restore justice to the land.

One evening, Will Scarlet ran up.

"Robin!" he cried. "Bad news! King Richard has been captured!"

"What?" frowned Robin. "By whom?"

Will said he didn't know, but that he was imprisoned in a castle far away. His captor said he would release him when England paid 100,000 pounds of silver as a ransom for setting the king free.

"Right," said Robin firmly, "we'll help raise the money, won't we, lads?"

The forest echoed to the cries of "Aye!"

Now that the outlaws had agreed to help King Richard, Robin collected half their store of money. They sold all the arms, fine clothes, and jewels they had stolen and added that money to the pile.

Robin sent the ransom money to London under strong guard. With it went a note written on the skin of a deer: *From Robin Hood and the honest men of Sherwood Forest. This is for their beloved King. They hope God will soon free him from his enemies abroad and at home.*

After this, Robin sent to London half of all the money he took. Thanks to such generosity, King Richard was quickly freed. He speedily returned to England.

Soon after he landed, the king began to hear stories of Robin Hood. Had a rich young lady given up her lands to live in Sherwood Forest with this outlaw? Was it true that he took  the law into his own hands and punished those who did wrong? Did he really rob the rich to pay the poor?

When the answer to all these questions was yes, Richard decided he must go to Sherwood Forest and meet this extraordinary Robin Hood fellow.

King Richard did not hear only praise for Robin Hood. The brother of Sheriff Murdach said Robin was a murderer, and the monks called him a thief. The king was eager to learn the truth.

Wherever he went, he asked about Robin Hood and his men. The rich knew only that he lived in Sherwood Forest; the poor shrugged and said nothing. They would not betray their friend.

The king tried a new tactic. Having heard that Robin robbed rich monks, he dressed himself as an abbot. He put his companions in monks' clothes and set off through the forest.

The plan worked splendidly.

They had not gone far when Little John stepped out in front of them. "Stop!" he cried, raising his bow.

The monks obeyed. Robin Hood now appeared, saying, "Good Abbot, hand over your money, and we will let you continue in peace."

"I've only forty pounds," replied the king. "The rest I spent looking for the king. But I'll willingly hand over what I have."

"Well said!" cried Robin. "An honest abbot at last! And one who loves the king, too. I won't search your saddlebags, and I invite you to feast with us in the forest."

The friendly abbot—King Richard—accepted Robin Hood's invitation to feast with him. They ate deer killed by the outlaws (against the law!), and they drank wine stolen from monks and merchants.

The king said nothing. He was watching and listening, making up his own mind about Robin Hood and his band.

When the meal was over, Robin suggested an archery competition. Whoever missed the target would get their ears boxed by Robin. The men laughed and agreed to the idea.

Several missed the small tree at which they were aiming, and each one received a hit from their leader. But Robin grew careless, missing the target himself.

"Well," he grinned, "who's going to give me a blow?" He looked around. "Come on,

Abbot," he said cheerily, "what about you?'"

"All right," said the warrior king, getting to his feet. "This is not what abbots normally do—but take that!"

His huge first smashed into Robin and sent him spinning to the ground.

At that moment, Sir Richard at the Lee and Marian arrived. The abbot's hood had slipped back on his head—the knight recognized him immediately. "Robin!" he cried. "Kneel! It's the king!"

Robin trembled at the feet of his king. How foolish he'd been not to recognize him! What fate now awaited them?

"I want the truth," said the king sternly.

"You shall have it, sire," answered Robin.

"Good. Then, tell me: Did you and your men kill Roger de Longchamp, Ivo le Ravener, Sir Ranulf de Greasby, Sir Ector de Malstane, Sir Philip de Scrooby, Sheriff Murdach, Sir Scrivel of Catsty, and others like them?"

"We did, my lord."

"Did you mock the Abbot of St. Mary's and steal his money?"

"We did, my lord."

"Did you give money to the poor and collect huge sums for my ransom?"

"We did, my lord."

King Richard smiled. "Then, stand up

Robin Hood and your merry men! You may have broken the law, but you acted for justice. I pardon you all."

At that, the outlaws cheered the king. He took aside Alan-a-Dale and Alice, and Robin Hood and Maid Marian. "You married without my permission," he said, "But I see you are made for each other. So, I have great pleasure in announcing that your marriages have my wholehearted approval!"

CHAPTER 6

The Last Arrow

On King Richard's command, Robin
and Marian received back the Malaset
lands that had been stolen from them.
They lived as a lord and lady should live,
treating all men and women with an even
hand. In all the land, "Squire Robin" was
known as a fair and honest man.

Meanwhile, many of the outlaws
went with the king when he returned to
France. There, some died, as did the king.
Those who came home—Little John, Will
the Bowman, Will Scarlet, and Much the
Miller's son—settled on Robin's lands.

King Richard was killed before he could
return to get rid of the nest of vipers near
Sherwood Forest. From time to time, Sir

Isenbart de Belame, Sir Guy of Gisborne, Baldwin the Killer, and Sir Roger of Doncaster met to plot the downfall of the man they still called "wolf's head."

For long years, they schemed. Finally, sixteen years after King Richard's death, their chance came. Robin had left home to fight a band of robbers. When he returned, he found his castle half burned and many of those inside slain.

Fearing the worst, Robin ran to Marian's room. There she lay, her hands neatly folded on her lap—dead.

Sorrow swallowed up Robin like a great wave. For a long time, he knelt and prayed for the soul of his dead wife. Then, he stood and asked in a calm, cold voice, "Who did this terrible deed?"

"A fiend," replied a maid, red-eyed with weeping. "A fiend named Sir Isenbart de Belame of Evil Hold. He shot

her even as she was talking with him."

"Thank you," said Robin. "That is all I need to know."

From all around, men came to his aid. Among them were Alan-a-Dale, Sir Herbrand, Ket the Trow, Hob o' the Hill, other surviving members of his outlaw band, and many more who loathed the very name of de Belame. All were willing to die to see justice done.

Robin led his army to the edge of the moat surrounding Evil Hold. "Come out and surrender, de Belame, you murderer!" he cried.

"Come and get me, wolf's head," sneered de Belame. "If you and your feeble rabble are strong enough."

"They are—and I promise we will," replied Robin.

Immediately, he gave orders for attacking the castle. The only way, he declared, was to cross the moat, hack down the drawbridge, and smash the portcullis.

Never was there such a siege as that of Evil Hold. It became the stuff of legends, and minstrels sang of it for many generations to come.

They told of how Robin's men, under a rain of arrows, crossed the moat on rafts and attacked the drawbridge with axes; of how the chains holding the drawbridge were cut, and a mighty oak brought as a battering ram; and how the portcullis was finally smashed open, and Robin's men poured into the castle.

No mercy was asked for, and no mercy shown. Some were cut down by swords; others were burned by boiling oil poured down from the battlements. The cobblestones of the castle courtyard ran red with the blood of battle.

In the midst of it all, Robin Hood and Little John fought together. Forward they went, cutting down their enemies on either hand. Their target was simple: Sir Isenbart de Belame, the murderer of the fair Maid Marian. Eventually, at the base of a tower, they cornered him.

"Wait!" called Robin, as Little John raised his great halberd above his head. "This villain must die as a criminal, not as a warrior. Bind him, and take him away!"

Two prisoners were taken during that terrible siege: Sir Isenbart de Belame and Baldwin the Killer. As they were led out in chains, the mob howled against them.

"Baldwin blinded my father!" cried one.

"De Belame was laughing when he killed Marian!" shouted another.

After a brief discussion, both men were hanged. Pitch and tar were then poured over Evil Hold, and the entire building was burned to the ground.

Robin could not face living in Malaset again. He gave the lands to a cousin and went to live in the forest once more. Here, with some of his old friends, he continued to help the weak and punish the wicked. Once again, the name of Robin Hood was on the lips of all who loved justice.

Of his foes, just two remained: Sir Roger of Doncaster and Sir Guy of Gisborne. Robin caught up with the latter one misty morning. It was a fair fight, and the better man won: Sir Guy of Gisborne finally got his just deserts from the point of Robin Hood's sword.

That left only Sir Roger of Doncaster. He was now an old man—but he still had a treacherous tongue.

Robin's deeds during his second spell in the forest would fill a whole new book. But time moved on. As the years passed, he grew weaker, and his eyes lost its sparkle.

All the while, Sir Roger of Doncaster waited. Every few months, he noticed, Robin called on his cousin, a nun in Kirklees Abbey. Slipping into the abbey

at night, Sir Roger whispered in the ear
of Dame Ursula, the abbess in charge: If
Robin Hood should die, the abbey might
receive thirty acres of good land …

Robin visited the abbey a week later.
He told Dame Ursula that he felt unwell,
and she invited him to rest. As was the
treatment in those days, she opened a
vein in his arm to let out some blood.
But she did not close it up. As Robin
slept, the blood continued to flow.

Fearing that something was wrong, Little John broke down the abbey door and rushed in. "Too late, dear John," whispered Robin. "I am gone. Pray, hand me my bow, and open the window."

With one final effort, Robin shot an arrow into the forest. "Where it has landed," he gasped, "dig my grave. There will I lie." And so it was done.